A PENGUIN MYSTERY

THIS NIGHT'S FOUL WORK

Fred Vargas was born in Paris in 1957. A historian and archae-
ologist by profession, she is a number-one bestselling author in
France. She is the author of eight novels featuring Commissaire
Jean-Baptiste Adamsberg, including *Wash This Blood Clean from
My Hand*, also available from Penguin. Her books have been
published in thirty-three countries and have sold more than
four million copies.